Sky

Peter

CAN

sky color

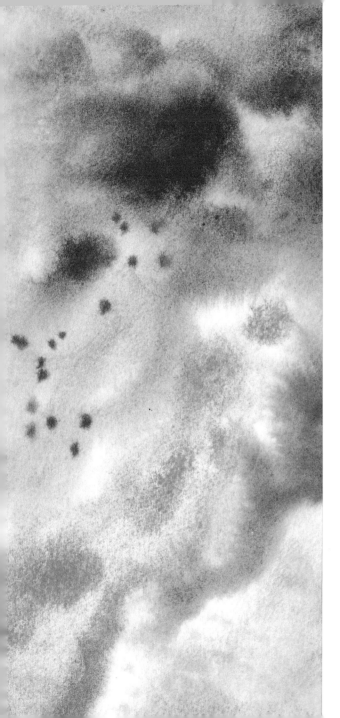

Marisol was an artist. She loved to draw and paint, and she even had her very own art gallery.

Not all her art hung in a gallery.
Much of it she shared
with the world.

She painted posters
to share ideas she
believed in.

At school, Marisol was famous for
her creative clothes, her box of art supplies,
and her belief that everybody was an artist.

Yes, Marisol was an artist through and through. So, when her teacher told the class they were going to paint a mural for the library, Marisol couldn't wait to begin.

The classroom buzzed with the sound of brainstorming. The students talked and sketched. Together they made a great big drawing.

Then they marched to the library.
"I'll paint a fish!" "I'll paint one, too."
"I'll paint the ocean!"
Marisol shouted, "I'll paint the sky!"

Marisol rummaged through the box
of paint but could not find any blue.

"How am I going to make the sky without blue paint?"

The bell rang. It was time to put their brushes down for the day. As she climbed aboard the bus, Marisol kept wondering.